50 0494107 5

D0297020

dream
d

C

THE MIDNIGHT DOLL

THE
MIDNIGHT DOLL

Maggie Glen

UWE, BRISTOL

3 JUL 1997

Library Services

HUTCHINSON
London Sydney Auckland Johannesburg

In the darkness of the corner
In its gloomy dusty darkness
Stands Susannah in a cupboard
In a cupboard never opened.

She is old and very fragile
Far too precious to be handled
Standing in her tattered satins
With her hair in matted tresses.

Long ago the one who made her
Made her for a children's playmate.
Oh, how sad they'd be to see her
Lonely, solemn-eyed and dreaming
In the cupboard's dusty darkness.

No small children — no more laughter
Just great-grandma slowly knitting
In the quiet by the fireside
With her needles and their clicking
And the tabby softly purring.

Now she sees someone is coming
Skipping, running up the pathway
And behind her comes her mother
Bringing flowers for great-grandma.

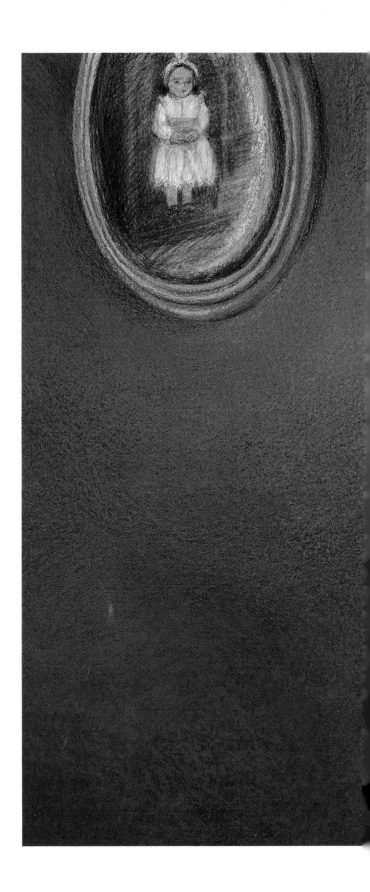

Oh, how long the grown-ups chatter
Long throughout the summer evening
Till the shadows grow like giants
Till the little girl grows restless
And she wanders to the corner.

Now Susannah sees her looking
Looking, staring at the cupboard
Sees her climbing upwards to her
Feels those small warm hands around her.

Then great-grandma turns and sees her
Sees her lifting down Susannah
Sees her press her gently to her
Asking, 'Was she yours, great-grandma?'
'Yes,' great-grandma whispers softly.

'We must keep her in the cupboard
Though you love her just as I do.
She is old and very fragile
Far too precious to be handled
And we would not wish to harm her.'

All too soon the front door closes
And the footstep sounds grow fainter.
Still and silent stands the cottage
Silent as the deepest forest.

Susannah once again is lonely
Sad and lonely in the cupboard
In its dusty gloomy darkness
Only spiders for companions
And the little woodworm beetles.

Deep inside her grows a longing
Grows a longing for a playmate
And Susannah in the cobwebs
Dreams a dream of great adventure.

And the tabby by the fireside
Eyes a-glowing like the embers
Sees the little doll Susannah
Make a knotted rope of ribbons.
Then, with small hands all a-tremble
Clinging to the silken sashes
She is slipping, sliding downwards.

By the door she stands and ponders
Ponders on the moon's great roundness
Sees the vastness of the dark sky
And its blackness pierced with starlight.
All the strangeness of the night-time
Fills the little doll with wonder.

All the little hidden creatures
Hidden deeply in the bushes
Hidden safely in the darkness
Call a shrill and sudden warning
Call, 'Oh little doll run swiftly
Hide with us from Moon-faced Hunter
Hide with us among the shadows.'

But too late she hears their warning
Hears the whirring of the wing beats
Feels the chill wind of their beating
Feels the talons close around her
Feels the great bird lift her skywards.

High above the park and houses
High above the very tree tops
Flies the fearsome midnight hunter
And Susannah flying with him.

Then she shouts and screams in anger
Screams, 'Oh let me go, you monster!'
Screams until the owl is startled
And his deadly talons loosen.

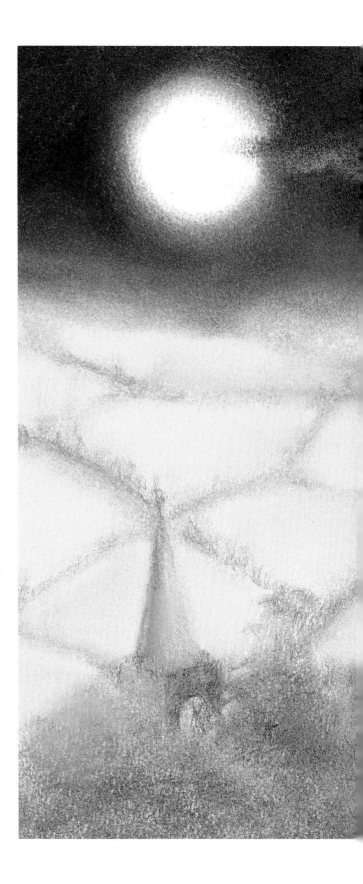

Slowly downwards floats Susannah
Spinning like a leaf in autumn
Till her feet touch something softly
Till she nestles deep in ivy
That fringes round the lighted window.

Warm inside a child is sleeping
Dreaming dreams of times forgotten
Dreams of drowsy summer evenings
And of secret garden places.

Now Susannah with a tapping
Wakens up the little sleeper
Who, while yawning, turns and sees her
At the window, shyly peeping
Lets her in and holds her closely
Filled with happiness at meeting.

On the counterpane by moonlight
Midnight dancing, twirling, leaping
Warmth of far-off times returning
Such a happy, joyful feeling
Susannah and her new friend laughing
Dance and play instead of sleeping.

In the quiet of the sunrise
In the misty grey-blue morning
Comes the moment for returning.
Susannah climbing down the ivy
Hears her new friend softly whisper
'Come back soon, my little dancer.'

Small, beneath the giant hedges
Swiftly through the dewy grasses
Susannah running, hurries homeward.

Safely back inside the cupboard
Damp with dewdrops stands Susannah
Stands as she has always stood there
But without a trace of sadness
Just a look that hints at laughter
And a smile that shares a secret
With the tabby by the fireside.

For my father

First published in 1996

1 3 5 7 9 10 8 6 4 2

© *Maggie Glen 1996*

Maggie Glen has asserted her right under
the Copyright, Designs and Patents Act, 1988,
to be identified as the author of this work

First published in the United Kingdom in 1996 by
Hutchinson Children's Books
Random House UK Limited
20 Vauxhall Bridge Road, London SW1V 2SA

Random House Australia (Pty) Limited
20 Alfred Street, Milsons Point, Sydney
New South Wales 2061, Australia

Random House New Zealand Limited
18 Poland Road, Glenfield
Auckland 10, New Zealand

Random House South Africa (Pty) Limited
PO Box 337, Bergvlei, South Africa

Random House UK Limited Reg. No. 954009

A CIP catalogue record for this book
is available from the British Library

ISBN: 0 09 176218 9

Printed in Hong Kong